Published by BAPM Pι
Copyright © 2019 by Bridgette Moody

ISBN: 978-1-7100-1501-0

All scriptures, unless otherwise noted, are taken from the New International Version of the Holy Bible.

Editorial Contribution and Book Design:
Bridgette Moody-Bridgette Moody Consulting/
www.bridgettemoody.com
bridgette@bridgettemoody.com

Cover Graphics & Design:
Adrienne Brown: distinguishdesingz@gmail.com

Printed in the United States of America

Library of Congress Literary Work
No.1-8314449191

DEDICATION

I dedicate this work to every person (that's you) who is gifted, and you have not been able to truly walk in your purpose. You have not carried out your purpose due to something you experienced in your life which caused you pain and made you feel inadequate. If you have experienced or are currently experiencing issues associated with feeling abandoned, broken, offended, rejected, having trust issues, have misguided expectations, or as result of any or all you feel like you are damaged goods. I want you to encourage you... do not abort the GIFT on the inside of you. Please allow yourself to heal and walk in your purpose. I made it through, so can you. You are more than a conquer. I believe in you, you can WIN!!!

Bridgette~

ACKNOWLEDGEMENTS

I am thankful and grateful for the revelation and the inspired word to share this work with the world and certainly in the Kingdom God. I want to thank my circle for their encouragement and for the persons who have allowed me to speak into their lives. I want to personally acknowledge Pastor Isaac & Lady Janet Pitre for their prayers and the opportunity to share the project in message which sealed the final work for this project. I am truly grateful.

I am thankful to my daughter, "Brea" who was instrumental in this work coming together (Love you)! I am thankful to God for the next level of understanding and for the experiences that are yet to be revealed as a result of the obedience to say yes and yield to what He spoke to my spirit. Thank you to my graphic designer, she gave life to my vision for this work; Adrienne Brown you are amazing! Thank you!

Gift

Aborted

CONTENTS

INTRODUCTION

The saying is "The things you will not confront, you will not change". When I was growing up, we were taught how to get past, get around, move past and move forward from the issues we were challenged with rather than facing them. We did not deal with the results of the behavior or the circumstances and situations we often stood in the face of; in truth, it was a false sense of strength. The strength is characterized as false because the day will come when you must face it and stand in your truth. If not, you will find yourself going in circles your entire life!

I strongly believe I was given this perspective from which to write to help individuals in taking the opportunity to self-evaluate and do some self-inventory. The process of facing the things which have caused you to constantly abort and never being able to give birth to your purpose is simple. Own the fact that "It" is, now is the time to let it go, forgive, confront it and have the conversation. It may be a conversation with you, it may be a conversation with someone else or it may just be a conversation with God.

Contrary to whom the conversation is with, it is time to have the dialogue. Confronting something that runs deep is like taking a shot. It may sting at first, but it will subside, and you will be able to move forward with life!

Phil 4:8 says, *"Finally, brothers and sisters, whatever is true, whatever is noble, whatever is right, whatever is pure, whatever is lovely, whatever is lovely, whatever is admirable-if anything is excellent or praiseworthy-think about such things."* It is time to get up, speak up and free up your mind, body and spirit! John 15:1-2 talks about how pruning produces fruit; Jesus says, *"I am the tree vine, and my father is the gardener. He cuts off every branch in me that bears no fruit, while every branch that does bear fruit, he prunes so that it will be even more fruitful."* The message in this scripture is important and a valuable lesson. Often, we are not producing fruit or walking in purpose because we need to rid ourselves of some things, feelings, and emotions. To prune means to trim by cutting away dead or overgrown branches or stems, it is vital to increase fruitfulness.

We have all been dealt a hand of life that may or may not be the ideal hand. It is not about what is in the hand you have been dealt, but more importantly, how the hand is played. Some of us struggle with playing the hand because of the experiences we have faced in life. I want to encourage you to play the hand to the best of your ability and win with what you have.

Life is more than going to a job, having a place to live and driving a nice car. Life is about experiencing new things, going new places and meeting new people. It is also about learning new cultures and adapting to change and making adjustments. Sometimes when we evolve, it helps us to resolve our unresolved issues in life. Allow your life and your purpose to impact the life of someone else positively.

Life is a journey, but when it is complicated and frustrating it makes the journey even harder to handle. There are several things that causes us to be distracted as well as derailed. Some distractions or derailments have no tangible connection, but it certainly has an emotional attachment.

If you will allow yourself to think honestly about your life situations and circumstances, there is some sort of emotional event that has caused you to experience a delay in getting to where it is you thought you should be by now. When carefully considered, the journey of your life can be traced to find where derailments took place and likely in part what caused those turn of events in your life. In some cases, the distraction was not caused by you, but it was received through the emotions you felt as a result of what happened during your life. In this book "Gift Aborted", I want to explore some areas that not only causes us pain, but it also robs us of our purpose in life.

Often, we are so taken back by the things which have happened in our life that we never evaluate the results of the impact once the dust has settled. It is my heart's desire you will allow this encouragement to spark onward thinking of your purpose. Whether you have been robbed of your purpose in whole or in part, the hope is "Gift Aborted" will offer to you your healing, your release, and your opportunity to rebuild your path to purpose.

Every action has a corresponding reaction and everything that is now grown had an inception. There is a root to everything we experience in life even though it appears the gift did not blossom into a beautiful tree or into a beautiful flower. If the root is properly cared for and evaluated, the results can always be different. I want to encourage you not to give up on the gift that is on the inside of you. I certainly plead with you not to allow your purpose to be derailed and unfulfilled. You have a legacy inside of you. A legacy that will remain long past your days on earth. Release yourself to live your life and discontinue the traditional method of just existing and getting by.

If you nurture the gift, unwrap the gift, and represent your gift, you can experience a maximized life. A gift is a natural ability or talent for which we are born with. Each of us were born with a gift and in some cases more than one. Because it is a gift you are graced with, you have an unexplainable passion for the area for which you are gifted. The gift that resides on the inside of you is your legacy and your inheritance.

As a result of just living life, we become conditioned to live a certain way because it is familiar and comfortable. Please understand, your gift is purposed to impact the life of not only you but someone else. There is somebody somewhere waiting on you to execute your gift and walk in your purpose. Do not allow the experiences or issues in life you have faced be your excuse to not walk in your purpose. Relocate your energy, stay alert, stay awake, and stay focused. Your purpose was created to be powerful and impact the world.

The gift is carried, but the purpose is never born...

Chapter 1
ABANDONED

What does it mean to be abandoned? To be abandoned means to be left feeling deserted or casted off. When did you experience it? Think about the time in your life for which you felt the abandonment. You may have been abandoned by a parent or felt abandoned as a result of someone you felt needed to be there and they were not there. In some cases, abandonment happens when people are physically present in your life, however; they do not know how to be there for you emotionally. It leaves you feeling alone with no one to share your heart and concerns with not to mention your life.

It is important to confront the feelings of being abandoned. If the feelings are not dealt with it can leave you searching for who you are as an individual and the reason you exist. It will lead to you not operating in your God given purpose. Ask the real questions to yourself and if you have the opportunity ask the question to the person to whom you feel abandoned you and ask why.

The reason it is relevant to have the conversation is because it will help you to understand the behavior and why the person or persons behaved the way they did. The question is how did being abandoned make you feel? What are the emotions you feel when you think about the person who abandoned you? It is an automatic and natural reaction when you think about being abandoned; the emotions are all negative and the feelings have no perception of positive intent. For a long time as a child I felt abandoned. I often wondered about how I ended up being the child that was raised by my great-grand mother.

Many thoughts ran through my mind over the years, I would try to justify and come up with a good strong reason as to why my mother gave me to my great-grand mother to raise. In the process of time, I came to understand why I ended up being raised by my great-grand mother of whom I affectionately called "Momma". I called her "Momma" because she was the mother figure in my life for many years even though I knew my biological Mother. My "Momma" taught me everything I knew about the fundamentals of life.

She taught me to cook at the age of eight years old. During that time, the art of cooking was at its finest because all cooking was from scratch. There were no recipes used. The recipe was a dash of that, a pinch of this, and a handful of the other. It was not until I was a young adult I truly began to understand. I began to understand why I was the one who was raised by "Momma". I learned it was not for the reason I was not good enough or my mother did not want me, but it was the best thing for me at that time.

My mother gave birth to me at the age of 16 which means she did not know a lot about being a mother at that time. It was about 11 months later my brother was born. As a result, it was in her best interest to have me be raised by my great-grand mother. Not only was it in the best interest of my mother, but it was also in my best interest and it was a part of my purpose in life. There were things I learned and was taught as a child I may have otherwise never known. My love for God and respect for who he is in my life is one of the ultimate things I drew from my childhood rearing.

I did not just feel abandoned by my mother for some period of time, but I also felt abandoned by my father.

While I knew who my father was, there was never a consistent relationship. For many years, I dealt with the feelings of abandonment not knowing what God was doing at the time. Because I did not know and did not understand, it caused me to struggle emotionally but also it made me a very independent person. My feelings and perspective became focused on learning how to take care of myself. The enemy is always looking for a way to derail us, get us off course, and cause us to lose focus of who we are and who he is. As a result, his job is to show us all the negative things about our life and the people who are a part of it. But God had another plan for our life. In John 10:10 Jesus says, "*The theft comes only to steal and kill and destroy; I have come that they may have life and have it to the full.*"

Abandonment also encompasses fear which leads to anxiety especially when people are face with the idea or thought of losing someone they are about. The experience of losing someone could be of several types, such as death, a relationship, a job, etc. Some of the other feelings or emotions that come along with abandonment include; forgotten, void, neglected, castaway, discarded, and the list goes on. How you feel often depends on the situation which occurred or the circumstances under which you were abandoned.

For myself, during the times of feeling like there was something wrong with me or I did not fit in, there was also the feeling of being ignored as well as forgotten. In addition, from my siblings I felt deserted and in all actuality; I really did not fit in. While I did not understand it at the time, God was preparing me even at that stage of life to have expectations of being something different and doing something different. In the process of developing this independent prospective to cope with the reality, I was also dealing with the feeling of being abandoned or thrown away so to speak. As a result, I never wanted to allow people to get to close not realizing why. I inadvertently had an underlined anxiety that was attached to the feelings of abandonment and all that went along with it, which was people would always walk away or leave.

Without knowing it, we carry the experiences and the feelings of childhood into adulthood, oftentimes; we do not realize what is happening until it gets to a point of being too much. Different emotions in our life causes different actions and corresponding action events in our lives. Many who have issues of abandonment also experience the following fears and anxieties:

- *Fear of intimacy* - *you go from one relationship to another relationship. You never commit because you want to find a reason to leave before the other person leaves you or you simply self-sabotage out of fear of feeling too deeply.*

- *Fear of being alone* – *you cling to and will not let go, you stay in relationships that are not healthy and draining. In some cases, there is a desire to leave but the abandonment issue will not allow you to exit. As a result, you become incarcerated by your fear.*

- *Act irrationally for no reason* – *this is when you basically self-sabotage relationships by hurting the other person or pushing them away to protect your own emotions and your heart. You ultimately cast false blame.*

- *Emotional securities- constantly needing reassurance, wanting emotional guarantees from the persons in your life and quite frankly anyone who will give it. It is a constant need to feel loved and appreciated.*

It is important to assess these areas of your life thoroughly, so you can determine the approach for making your way through it and be able to forgive the person or persons in order to get healing for your life.

You do not want to allow abandonment to be the low cloud that controls your life, where we go, what we do, and how you do it. Consequently, it is in our best interest to ensure we dispel the risks of neglect, stress, anxiety, and trauma related issues in our life. It becomes necessary as soon as you know you are dealing with issues of abandonment that you find out the best way to deal with the emotions. First, it is essential for you to establish emotionally healthy relationships and establish healthy emotional boundaries. You need to know how to handle old emotions and feelings when they surface.

How do you remedy the response of yesterday with a response of love and forgiveness today? You must face the issues that have haunted you and caused you pain and disappointment. Your life depends on you forgiving the persons who abandoned you.

Next, seek help for yourself, therapy is not a bad word nor is it so expensive you cannot afford it. There are different types of therapy that will help you to release the hurt, the frustration, the disappointment, and the pain. One form of inexpensive therapy is journaling. Purchase a journal and get a pen that makes you happy and write every time you feel the emotions coming up in your mind or your heart. Write down how the person who abandoned you made you feel. I suggest writing about the one you feel abandoned you whether it has been corrected, confronted, or dealt with face to face, it is important for you to release the emotions that keep you incarcerated with the fear of being abandoned.

Lastly, take care of yourself by making sure your needs are met emotionally. Make sure you have and are in healthy relationships. Toxic relationships and friendships should be avoided like the plague. Free yourself to be yourself wholly and unapologetically. If you find yourself in a place of feeling like you have never forgiven the person who you feel abandoned you, take a moment and say this prayer. I believe God will help you to forgive and free them in your heart.

God, I ask that you help me to forgive the person who abandoned me. I pray for them and I ask to help me to love them despite how being abandoned has made me feel. God, I trust you with my heart and I trust you with my life. You made them both and you know how to heal and fix them both at the same time. God, I trust you that I am healed, I am delivered, and I am set free. Amen!

Self-Evaluation – Abandoned/Abandonment

1. When were there times in life you felt abandoned?

_____

_____

_____

_____

_____

_____

2. Have you had a conversation with the person or persons of whom you feel abandoned you? Or faced the situation that left you feeling abandoned?

_____

_____

_____

_____

_____

_____

_____

3. Did you ask the questions that have always lingered in your heart?

_____

_____

_____

_____

_____

_____

_____

Grace Check:
If you have not already…

Can you find it in your heart to forgive and let it go? Search yourself deeply with this question and pen your true feelings. It will help you with healing.

_____

_____

_____

_____

_____

_____

_____

Jot the immediate thoughts that come to mind whereas feeling **abandoned** concerns you… then **JOURNAL** about each thought you jotted down. *(Jotting is a word or quick phrase- Journaling is writing complete thoughts about what you jotted)*

_____

_____

_____

_____

_____

_____

_____

_____

_____

_____

_____

_____

_____

_____

_____

_____

_____

_____

Chapter 2
BROKENNESS

There are different seasons and times in our life, whereas we experience different things and those experiences affect us in different ways. Being broken to me means to have something happen to you emotionally and it breaks you down in your spirit. The brokenness causes you to not be able or have the capacity to encourage yourself, to motivate yourself or even care for yourself.

A state of brokenness is a serious thing and it affects us emotionally, mentally, and spiritual in a way that someone tangible hitting or beating you does not match up to, I mean it does even come close. When your soul is detached from your spirit and your ability to will yourself to positive thinking or rise above the fact you have been broken, it is a surmountable feeling to overcome. When you are spiritually broken it is also a dark place and it is difficult to bring light into the space. Brokenness brings on a level of stress and depression you never see coming. By the time you realize what is happening you are weeks and months into a state of mental breakdown. There is a constant flow of what is wrong with me; why was I not good enough; what did I do wrong; why is this happening to me? The list goes on based on the type of hurt that broke you, for all of us it is something different.

We never think in the moment of being broken and feeling all the negative emotions that the brokenness happened to help us heal and find our purpose. I lived on broken pieces for many years. When going through my season of brokenness, I never once found it purposeful. It was quite the contrary, I thought it was one of the most horrific times of my life. I was in ministry at the time and I ministered every Sunday, broken. It helped me to maintain my sanity and continue to be a mother to my children. However, in the process of time it all caught up to me and just about took me out. I was literally dying from the inside out. It was all unfolding because I was so very broken, and I had never stopped to deal with and face my brokenness. Brokenness is a real place with real consequences and real circumstances. I lived on broken pieces for so long until brokenness became wholeness in disguise. I simply learned to live as a broken person and for many years it was my new normal. I was financially ruined, emotionally distraught, weakened, infirmed and dysfunction was at its' highest peak as I attempted to continue to function spiritually. I felt for a long time I was living in a shattered glass and if anybody got too close, said the wrong thing, or even hugged me on the wrong day, I would just break.

During the time I was going through my state of brokenness, it was extremely severe. The situation I went through, I went through it publicly so there was no question as to what caused me to be broken at least in part, it was known in the community of which I lived. In addition to being broken and experiencing the situation publicly, God went public through me every week. While in a marriage that was experiencing some turbulence, my brokenness was on display because there was still purpose for my life. I later came to know it was the glory of God being revealed through my life. God' glory was revealed I publicly through my life and He did it each week through my praise and through my worship, all while being broken. In addition to God going public through me in this way, it was not just a state of brokenness; I was gracefully broken. Grace is known as the unmerited favor of God, favor that only he can provide. Gracefully broken translates being broken by God for God's purpose, which means he takes your situation and uses it for his glory and then he can take you to a new level in him. I found out we are sometimes broken to be promoted and elevated without any opposition or question. It is amazing when you think about brokenness, when one person is broken in a home the home is broken, especially if it is the mother. Mothers are usually the glue that holds it all together. As a result, there are broken children and then a broken family and lastly a broken home. We must understand and know God is always with us to help mend us back together physically, emotionally, and spiritually. Psalm 34:18 confirms for us, *"The Lord is close to the brokenhearted and He saves those who are crushed in spirit. 1 John 3:20 says, "For whenever our hear condemns us, God is greater than our heart, and he knows everything". "Isaiah 40:8 declares, "The grass withers and the flowers fades, but the word of God will stand forever. Yet I am not alone, for my Father is with me."*

Despite what I experienced in my place of brokenness; I was blessed as a result. I begin to rely and trust God on a level I had not done before. I am a witness God will never leave us nor forsake us, He is always there for us anytime, anyplace, and under all circumstances. God proved himself to me during my plight of brokenness. God showed up as Jehovah Jireh, he provided everything I needed. He showed up as Jehovah Nissi, He was my banner and ultimately allowed me to be victorious. He then showed up as Jehovah Shalom and gave me an unexplainable and unforgettable peace.

I want to encourage you, you can make it on broken pieces, everyday allow yourself to put a piece back in place through facing the reality of what broke you in the first place. Next, put another piece in place by praying and sharing your heart with God. After praying, it is important to be open. Accept the help God provides for the purpose of helping you heal and forgive the person or the thing that caused you to brake in the first place. Often our position is to get broken, brake down, and then sit down in the brokenness.

We want to wallow in the hurt and feel sorry for ourselves and absorb the pain, when often; it does nothing for the hurt and pain we feel, except intensify it. We push ourselves deeper in that dark place hoping to somehow numb ourselves of feeling what is really happening. If you can pull yourself up to the surface and look out among you and around you, you will see you amid others that are also broken. In many cases, it is broken people who cause brokenness in the lives of others. Pray and ask God to help you heal from the place that has you broken. He is the potter and we are the clay and I believe God can put us back together again. I am inclined to believe we are better the second time around. As you complete this chapter think very intensely and truthfully about how brokenness has impacted your life and your purpose. If brokenness is an area for which you have experienced pain and derailment in your life, please say this prayer and invite God into the room of your heart and allow him to help you pick up the broken piece and mind them back together.

God, I pray you will come into my heart and help me to forgive the person or persons that caused be to brake. God help me to heal from the situation and the circumstance that caused me to feel broken and helpless. I need your love in my heart to help me sustain and maintain so that I can be a blessing. I need your strength to confront and face what hurt me and help me to move forward in victory. In Jesus Name, Amen!

Self-Evaluation – Brokenness

1. When have you felt Broken?

_____

_____

_____

_____

_____

_____

2. What are some situations you feel left you broken

_____

_____

_____

_____

_____

_____

_____

_____

3. If your state of brokenness involved someone else, have you had a conversation with the person?

_____

_____

_____

_____

_____

_____

_____

Grace Check:
If you have not already...

Can you find it in your heart to forgive and let it go? Search yourself deeply with this question and pen your true feelings. It will help you with healing.

_____

_____

_____

_____

_____

_____

_____

Jot the immediate thoughts that come to mind whereas feeling **broken** concerns you... then **JOURNAL** about each thought you jotted down. *(Jotting is a word or quick phrase- Journaling is writing complete thoughts about what you jotted)*

Chapter 3
OFFENSE

I have been in church all my life and the first time I heard the term "church hurt" I thought it was such an awful thing. I later found out through the experiences of life, it was more about people being offended by something someone said or did. Not only was this enlightening to me, but also I discovered people who deal with offense experience this feeling many times without anyone saying anything to them directly, calling their name, mentioning their address, or none of the kind, but it is from the place for which they perceive a thing to be true about them. A person can feel insulted, resentful, annoyed, hurt, or angered (or all the above) by something stated in their presence. People are offended for many reasons and most often it comes down to their perception or their point of view. It is all in how the person looks at what was done or how a person perceives something spoken.

It is true, a person's perception is also their reality. If a person believes a thing to be true, then it is true to them.

However, the reality can be a false reality because what is perceived and what is true are two worlds apart. When a person is easily offended, they are also easily made to feel uncomfortable, but based on their personal value being violated. Being offended has a lot to do with what a person has decided within themselves goes against what is approved of and agreed with and it is all self-contained because no one else knows but them. As a result, it causes the skin of such people to be extremely thin, which means they are very easily offended. The interesting thing about living with offense is the fact that one never stops to think about or ask the question, "Why am I so easily offended?" It is an important question and it truly deserves your attention. The disposition of offense can cause you to derail your life and keep you from experiencing success and fulfillment.

In an effort to help with getting offense out of your life and having a new perspective on how you perceive things, I would ask you to consider the following self-checks when you are feeling offended or when dealing with offense.

- *Whenever you are feeling offended, first understand your feelings and why you are feeling some kind of way. Is it truly about what someone said or is it that what the person said is actually true? What are your feelings and why are those feelings counteractive by someone you may possibly not know? What is the offense really about?*

- *Understand why the person is being offensive. Take a moment to digest what the person is saying, ask questions, and dialogue about what you are about to take offense to. It may be something is not directly about you and what is being said may have something to do with a situation or circumstance by no means related to you. Align the information being received appropriately before responding to your own offense rather than what is being said in the moment.*

- *Understand and recognize when a person is sharing constructive criticism. The statements shared by someone giving constructive criticism is not personal or meant to hurt or cause harm, but to be a help and uplift and make something or someone better.*

- *Understand and recognize when to just allow things to roll off your back. Breathe in and out and just meditate and clear your mind of thoughts that are toxic and non-productive.*

- *Take the opportunity and allow yourself to be exposed to different cultures and try some different things, such as driving through a different part of your city, traveling to a different state, going to a different church, attend a function your normally would not go to, listen to different kinds of music, and read different types of books or just begin to read period. Choose books that are culturally different, it will help to broaden your thinking and understanding.*

It is my hope the simple self-evaluation will help you to evolve in your thinking about yourself and about how others think of you. Oftentimes, offence happens when we have developed the world we want to live in and we live in it how we want, and on our terms; regardless of the situations, circumstances and conditions and it is simply unrealistic.

As a result, we have this self-centered view of the world and how we should function in it as an individual, so it keeps us enslaved to have everybody agree with us about everything and if not, our feelings are hurt. When you are easily offended, notice most times no one else knows you are offended because you are not their focus. There is no intentional act or action to hurt or offend you but because of the disposition you have elected to reside in, you feel personally disrespected and attacked.

When hurt happens to you by others who have no idea what your name is or that you exist, it means we have caused ourselves to feel certain emotions based on something that happened or did not happen and it has nothing to do with your current plight in life. The feeling of being humiliated or hurt most often comes from a place you never confronted and face physically to say, "you hurt me by what you said or by what you did." I would encourage you to take a moment and recall in your mind and in your heart the first time you felt offense or offended. Where were you when it happened? Who was present in your space when the emotion emerged? How were you humiliated or hurt? Why do you think you felt offended by what was said or done? Was it the person that made the difference of how you reacted emotionally? Or, was it how it was said that caused you pain? Find the root of your offence and you will find the remedy for healing your heart and restoring your emotional health.

It is important to heal in this area, so you do not continue to camouflage offence and pass it off as just not feeling good or feeling the environment or space you are challenged to function in. Take off the mask of offence and allow yourself to be emotionally freed so you can walk in your life's purpose and calling. Someone somewhere is waiting on you to do what it is you were created to do, born to fulfill, and gifted to birth, but offence is holding both you and the others hostage. Release yourself from the incarceration of offense or of being offended. There is a big world waiting on you! Press inward so that you can press onward and then press outward…your success is in the press!

Self-Evaluation – *Offense/Feeling Offended*

1. Under what circumstances and in what instances have you been offended?

_____

_____

_____

_____

_____

2. Have you ever been offended by a person of whom you have never met? Did you ask yourself how is it you were offended by a stranger?

_____

_____

_____

_____

_____

_____

3. Have you taken the time to evaluate what causes you feel insulted or offended and why?

_____

_____

_____

_____

_____

_____

Grace Check:
If you have not already…

Can you find it in your heart to forgive and let it go? Search yourself deeply with this question and pen your true feelings. It will help you with healing.

_____

_____

_____

_____

_____

_____

_____

_____

Jot the immediate thoughts that come to mind whereas feeling **offended** concerns you… then **JOURNAL** about each thought you jotted down. *(Jotting is a word or quick phrase- Journaling is writing complete thoughts about what you jotted)*

_____

_____

_____

_____

_____

_____

_____

_____

_____

_____

_____

_____

_____

_____

_____

_____

_____

_____

Chapter 4
REJECTION

We have all experienced at some point and time in our lives some level or form of rejection. When you think of rejection you think of being dismissed, turned down, shut out, excluded, ostracized, avoided, ignored or excommunicated. It is an emotional hurt that causes you to feel almost obsolete. Oftentimes, when a person says or does something that causes the feeling of rejection, they have no idea of how or what it makes you feel like. Depending on what you may be experiencing at the time of being rejected or made to feel rejected it can take you into a whirlwind of emotions for which it can take some time for you to recover. Rejection affects your self-esteem and makes you feel inadequate, less than, and a failure. Constant rejection can cause one to go into a deep state of depression and have severe anxiety. It is a real thing and it happens to the best of us, even in our everyday life just trying to be who we are - doing what it is that we do.

Depression and severe anxiety is a real problem in our society, and we must learn how to help ourselves and others who live with it. It is time to take back control of our lives, our emotions and our purpose in life. When we allow someone or something to control our mood, our mental state, and our physical abilities; we have given the person, the situation, or the circumstance too much power. It may require help to take back control, but I believe you can do it. If you are experiencing depression or severe anxiety as a result of being rejected at some point in your life, please get some help. If you are unsure if you are dealing with depression consider some of the following as potential signs of depression and if any are true for you, please see help.

- *Consistent sadness*
- *Self-hatred*
- *Loss of interest for basic activities of life*
- *Irritable*
- *Isolation*
- *Low self-worth*
- *Reduction in Energy to live life*

- *Restlessness – normal sleep pattern is impacted*

- *Negative change in eating habits or loss of appetite*

- *High-risk behavior*

- *Suicidal thoughts*

It is amazing how rejection can cause one to go into a state of depression, but it is happening every day. Staring these emotions in the face and finding out how you got to the place of depression is important. It is vital to your life's purpose to seek help. If you cannot talk about it, write about it. Put pen to paper and allow the emotions, the hurt, the pain, to be released through the pen to the paper and say what you need to say, how you need to say it, and how you feel about what you have experienced. Your purpose is buried in the rejection and the depression, resurrect it and live your life!

At some point, you must understand the rejection you are feeling and why you are feeling rejected. You must ask yourself the hard questions and then answer them.

This is one way to get to the place of healing and restoration. Who rejected you? How did it make you feel when you were rejected by this individual? Are you afraid to approach the object of your rejection? Why are you afraid? How long have you been living with the rejection? These are all important questions to ask yourself.

Doing this self-evaluation will help to build your confidence and face your object of rejection, even if it is just on paper. This self-evaluation is essential even if the object of your rejection is deceased. Release them and free yourself. While it may be the hardest thing you have ever considered doing, it will be one of the best things you could ever do for your life and for the opportunity for your true purpose to be born. If you are currently in a place of dealing with rejection, it is possible to salvage your emotional state of mind and change your disposition as well as your perspective. When you experience rejection by an individual, it is a good idea to walk away or take some time to step back and look at the situation to establish what is happening and why.

Allow yourself to feel all the emotions as it will help you to not hold on to negative feelings. At this point, I suggest changing the circle of people that you are around on a consistent basis. It is important to be surrounded by people who impact your life positively and speak life into you.

You should be around people who encourage you and who are honest with you and supportive all at the same time. Always seek ways to build yourself up when someone else has attempted to tare you down. Taking to the positive approach is not denying you have experienced being rejected, but it also gives you the opportunity to be accepted by someone else. The truth of the matter is … not everyone will accept you… will reject you. It is equally important to understand why the rejection happened.

Rejection sometimes occurs to help us not get distracted by something that will ultimately not be good for you in the first place. Try not to take every rejection personally, accept it as soon as possible and try to move on from it. When experiencing rejection, I have learned there was something about the situation or the individual that was not right for me.

In most cases, as time passed by, I found the assessment to be true. It was a false representation of integrity and real relationship and I was favored by being rejected. Whenever you are faced with a feeling of being unloved and rejected in your current comfort zone or circle of people, it is a good idea to meet new people. Many times, people become comfortable with you and they do not value the gift in you, however; meeting new people gives you the opportunity to get a fresh perspective on what others see in you. Likewise, it gives you an opportunity to see what you see in yourself.

When we take the opportunity to make some changes, we can make a change in our life. There is always comfort in the word of God when you are feeling unloved and unappreciated, not valued and your self-worth is challenged. **Jeremiah 31:3** says *"Yes, I have loved you with an everlasting love; therefore, with loving kindness, I have drawn you."* **Psalm 136:2** encourages us to *"Give thanks to the God of gods. His love endures forever."* People will come and go in your life, some relationships are for a season, some are for a reason, and others are for a lifetime, but the love of God is forever and always. **Isaiah 54:10** declares *"Though the mountains be shaken, and the hills be removed, yet my unfailing love for you will not be shaken nor my covenant of peace be removed, says the Lord who has compassion on you."* **John 15:13** confirms for us *"There is no greater love than to lay down one's life for one's friends."*

This is a confident reminder of how incomparable God's love is for us. **Lamentations 3:22-23** affirms *"Because of the Lord's great love, we are not consumed, for his compassions never fail. They are new every morning..."* **Psalm 52:8** instructs us *"Don't trust your feelings, instead rely totally on God's love that lasts forever and ever."* The love of God is sure, real, everlasting, and available to us in all and under all situations. There is nothing we could ever do or not do, say or not say that would cause us not to be eligible to receive God's love. We do not have to apply for God's love, we do not have to qualify for God's love, all we have to do is receive his love. Jesus Christ was despised and rejected, and He was acquainted with sorrow as well as grief, but he took on the sins of the world to redeem us from all such experiences. The love of God never fails, and he never gives up on us.... never!

I am encouraging you to address the rejection you have experienced, with love. Be open to being loved and assess the love that is currently being shown to you or shared with you.

Self-Evaluation – Rejection

1. Have you experience the feeling of rejection on more than one occasion? Was it personal or corporate?

_____

_____

_____

_____

_____

_____

2. Have you ever felt rejected by family? How did it make you feel?

_____

_____

_____

_____

_____

_____

_____

3. Have you been rejected by a friend? How did you handle the emotions of the rejection? Did you ever talk about your feelings?

_____

_____

_____

_____

_____

_____

Grace Check:
If you have not already…

Can you find it in your heart to forgive and let it go? Search yourself deeply with this question and pen your true feelings. It will help you with healing.

_____

_____

_____

_____

_____

_____

_____

Jot the immediate thoughts that come to mind whereas feeling **rejected** concerns you… then **JOURNAL** about each thought you jotted down. *(Jotting is a word or quick phrase- Journaling is writing complete thoughts about what you jotted)*

_____

_____

_____

_____

_____

_____

_____

_____

_____

_____

_____

_____

_____

_____

_____

_____

_____

_____

Chapter 5
TRUST

As I share and discuss the topic of trust, the question can be asked; what is it about the dialogue of this subject matter that crosses lines and identifies with the average person no matter what the background, ethnicity, or experiences? Well, the list for this response can go on and on. As I go deeper, I am sharing a large part of what I have dealt with for many years and ultimately, I had to look it in the face and confront the feelings which had controlled my life for so long, unaware. As children, the innocence of it all allows our heart to freely and easily trust the people who are in our life. What and who we are introduced to as children, we have no reason at the point and time to not trust it. As we mature, grow, experience life and situations, we begin to experience different emotions about different things and different people in our life based on the relationships. For me, it was my experience with my biological father. As a child, I would long for my father's presence.

I love my father to the extent that I just loved to hear my father's voice. Whenever he would call me on the phone, my eyes would just light up. It was a voice of authority, his voice was smooth and silky, he had a voice that was also calming and reassuring, however; I did not know it was also a voice that was deceiving. What do I mean by a voice of deception? As time would go on, my father would come to see me periodically, as I lived with my great-grandmother. He would sit and visit for a while or take me to the store or to visit other family members. Once we would arrive back at my great-grandmother's, he would tell me he would be back the next few hours or sometimes he would say the next day. Whatever the time frame would be, I would go and sit on the front steps of the porch of my great-grandmother's home and wait for him to return and of course, he never would. Many days my great-grandmother would come and tell me to come inside because night would have fallen by this time. I would return to the steps the next day, waiting for him to come back. I repeated this routine for many years because I trusted him to do and be what he said. Sometimes it would not only be days before he would return or call, on many occasions it would be months and often years. This went on until I was about fifteen years old. I had pretty much shut down by this time and gave up on ever having that relationship I so deeply longed for. Additionally, I shut down regarding any man be it father, brother, friend, etc. without realizing it. From the time I had the experience into adulthood, I had no real expectations of the men in my life. My perspective was all men were liars and would never be true to their word. The probability of me totally trusting a man was slim to none as a result. I carried it into my early relationships and by the time I was married I had just begun to deal with the pain and the hurt of what the behavior did to me emotionally.

I took the time to share with the husband to be at that time how fearful I was and the trust issues I had struggled with previously. I thought it was important for him to know where the issues stemmed from. Consequently, it was ultimately a reawaking of those feelings and mistrust as the marriage did not survive.

I realized at this point, I really needed to go to the root and resolve the matter. I begin to see how I would never get to my place of true happiness if I did not take the time to truly get free and delivered from the trust issues. The other perspective was to continue to tolerate the behavior but to also not have healthy relationships and thereby continue the pattern of hurt and disappointment. Ideally when you think of trust or the ability to trust someone, you think about how trust is defined as a firm belief in the reliability, the truth, the ability, or the strength of someone or something.

To add further depth to the expectation of trust, we place confidence, belief, faith, sureness, certainty, certitude, assurance, conviction, credence, and total reliance in the people we trust without evidence or investigation of them otherwise. Wow, what a special residence we give this type of individual in our life or in our heart. We give them the full responsibility, duty, or obligation of always being true to the heart for which we have given them a key. We trust these individuals to keep our heart safe, protected, and guarded.

We place a certain level of hope and or expectation in these individuals, because we trust them. As a little girl, I had every confidence, hope, and faith in the fact that every time my father would say, I will see in a little bit or I will call you in a little bit; he was good for it. My expectation was seeing him return or hearing the phone ring. In most cases, neither occurred and I was left holding on to the hope, the confidence, or faith the next time he would definitely show up and yet, the behavior continued to repeat itself over and over again.

As time proceed, I became a mother, a wife, a confidant and a friend with the mindset of never wanting anyone in my life to feel that sense of hurt and disappointment. It became my quest to be loyal and trustworthy whether it was a friend, my child, my sister or brother. I wanted it to be known you could depend on me. In the process of being loyal, dependable, reliable, trusting, and giving, I found myself being depleted because during it all I was trying to ensure I did not cause others to experience hurt or disappointment from me.

I was disappointing myself by not reaching deep within my inner self and finding out why I had this sense of wanting to be different and impact lives. As a result, I functioned for years not truly understanding my purpose in life and it was not fun at all nor was it truly fulfilling. What I ultimately realized is relationships require trust if they are to be meaningful, healthy, and long-lasting. It also means you can feel safe with the individuals you trust in your life.

In the process of time, I matured spiritually and emotionally and after going through a divorce realized, I had to confront the giant of trust in my life. At the age of 47, I got on a plane and flew across the country to spend some time with my biological father and to have a one on one conversation. After living life and experiencing love and commitment from others, I knew trust existed, but I never understood why it did not exist from him. Once I was able to sit face to face and ask the questions and listen to the answers looking into his eyes, I realized that my expectations of my father were misguided.

I learned my father did not have the capacity to be the father I desired to have as a little girl. As a result, I had to forgive the years of hurt and disappointment and come to the realization of who he was and who he was intended and purposed to be pertaining to my life. He was the introduction and catalyst for getting me to be a part of humanity. However, God used my "Dad" to be the example of hope, trust, faith, dependability, fortitude, and fight and for that I am truly grateful. I am more excited than ever for the new relationships I will build and for those I have been able to repair or rekindle as a result of trust. Will the repaired relationships be what I initially expected them to be, probably not; but they will be healthy and meaningful because I was able to conquer the "Trust Giant."

I want to encourage you to take the time to heal your heart and break free of what is preventing you from walking in purpose. Try having a conversation with the person who broke your trust. Take the opportunity to understand the depth of the broken trust. It is a tall task to come back from broken trust, but you can do it.

The affect it has on your ability to believe and have faith in another individual is challenging but it is definitely something you can overcome in time. It requires you being honest with yourself and learning how to share your truths and emotions and communicate them effectively. The honesty will help the other party understand how to best help build the area of your heart back to a place of vulnerability.

The restoration of trust is a beautiful thing. When you arrive back at a place of being able to trust, it is liberating, and it frees your heart to feel and to experience the simple things in relationships that are built on the simple but important factor of trust. The results of not being able to trust others and your self are unhealthy and draining. Take the time, do the work, and allow your heart to be restored and your faith to be renewed. I believe, if you can find your way to confront the hurt and the disappointment you can find the way to your purpose and live your best life!

Self-Evaluation- Trust

1. What areas do you have trust issues?

_____

_____

_____

_____

_____

_____

2. Who defied your trust? How did it make you feel? How did you handle it?

_____

_____

_____

_____

_____

_____

_____

_____

_____

3. What are you doing to restore your ability to trust again?

_____

_____

_____

_____

_____

_____

_____

Grace Check:
If you have not already…

Can you find it in your heart to forgive and let it go? Search yourself deeply with this question and pen your true feelings. It will help you with healing.

_____

_____

_____

_____

_____

_____

_____

Jot the immediate thoughts that come to mind whereas **trust** concerns you... then **JOURNAL** about each thought you jotted down. *(Jotting is a word or quick phrase- Journaling is writing complete thoughts about what you jotted)*

_____

_____

_____

_____

_____

_____

_____

_____

_____

_____

_____

_____

_____

_____

_____

_____

_____

_____

Chapter 6
EXPECTATIONS

We live our lives every day with some type of expectation being the basis for how we function. Let's take inventory of our expectations that are a part of our daily living. When we lie down at night, it is our expectation we will awake the next morning to start a routine, whatever it may be. We expect to get in our vehicles and drive to our places of employment or whatever it is you do each day. We expect our family and our children to behave and be productive citizens and participate in life's ordinary and we hope and pray they reach extraordinary. Likewise, we have an expectation our spouse or significant other will always be there to be what it is we need them to be to us and for us. In addition, we expect friends and those we work with to be loyal and committed to the relationships that have been established. We hold strong beliefs these things will happen or be the case for our immediate, near, and distant future.

The truth of the matter is things can change at any time and those expectations may or may not come to fruition. The expectations are expectations that are normal everyday life expectations, and no one would blame you for having either one of them as a project hope of something or someone. However, in life as we experience some of the emotional traumas previously mentioned, it is also normal to have low expectation not only of yourself but also of those who may be around you. I have learned over the years; it is important to understand our expectation and what it is we can expect from the people in our lives and who it is we can expect things from in our life.

Expectations are often directed based on our own capacity to live, to love, and to grow. It is important to understand our capacity and the capacity of others in our life is different. Without realizing this perspective, we often have misguided expectations of the people in our lives. The expectations are misguided because the capacity you have as an individual or the capacity for which you have grown to is not the same capacity for your spouse, children, sister, brother, mother, father, etc.

If we are not careful, we become distracted and frustrated because the levels of capacity do not match up. When there are arguments between lovers, spouses, friends, colleagues, etc. it is mostly contributed to different levels of expectations and capacity. When the indifference of capacity and expectation cross each other, there is bound to be frustration and disappointment. When this occurs, it behooves us to take the opportunity to trace it back and determine the level of capacity and pair the capacity with the level of expectation for which we have for the individual or situation. As we walk this path of life, it is essential to our emotional success to take inventory of the relationships in our lives. Evaluating our own capacity level and the expectations we have of ourselves will help us to determine the level of capacity and expectation of those we are in relationship with.

For example, I have three adult children and I have different expectations for each of them because each of them have different levels of capacities. Not only are the levels of capacity different but the expectations are different for all three of them respectfully.

Each of my children have different gifts, talents, and levels of maturity. As a result, the expectations I have of them are all different and based on their level of capacity. I have found as a result of knowing the expectation and being clear about it, our relationships are stronger and more cohesive, yet not perfect. Also, this is true for every other relationship in our life. Sometimes we are derailed, and we get off purpose or purpose is never the focal point, because we have mis-guided expectations of someone or something else fulfilling the role. We never realize the object of our expectation does not have or hold the capacity. The capacity for where you should be and can be is within you.

Mis-guided expectations are misleading for our emotional wellness as we believe falsely. We trust amiss because our expectations are not based on truth and the actual capacity of an individual, but more on what we want it to be. Evaluate your expectations and be certain they are appropriate for the situation and the relationship. You will thank me later! The point I really would like for you to understand and take away is, it is not that the person does not want to fulfill some of the expectation you may have of them. The point of the matter is they cannot provide what they do not possess. It matters not how much we want them to have it, be it or do it. A person can only give from what they have. Learn to accept the capacity they have to offer and pray regarding the void you may feel as a result. In time, you will understand their position is not their preference, but it is the purpose they have in your life!

Self-Evaluation- Expectations

1. Have you had expectations for something or of someone you have not acknowledged was mis-guided?

_____

_____

_____

_____

_____

_____

_____

2. If you have experienced having expectations of someone who did not deliver, did you consider the capacity for them to deliver?

_____

_____

_____

_____

_____

_____

_____

_____

3. Did you have a conversation regarding the expectations that disappointment you?

_____

_____

_____

_____

_____

_____

Grace Check:
If you have not already…

Can you find it in your heart to forgive and let it go? Search yourself deeply with this question and pen your true feelings. It will help you with healing.

_____

_____

_____

_____

_____

_____

_____

_____

_____

Jot the immediate thoughts that come to mind whereas handling **expectations** concerns you… then JOURNAL about each thought you jotted down. *(Jotting is a word or quick phrase- Journaling is writing complete thoughts about what you jotted)*

_____

_____

_____

_____

_____

_____

_____

_____

_____

_____

_____

_____

_____

_____

_____

_____

_____

_____

_____

Chapter 7
DAMAGED GOODS

Life throws curve balls. They are often unexpected and quite honestly, many times hard for us to manage catching. Some of the curve balls come labeled as abandonment, brokenness, offense, rejection, trust, mis-guided expectations, fear and the list goes on. When we are unable to catch the curve balls or when we fail to manage them appropriately, it leaves us feeling inadequate or impaired in some way. Or simply not good enough for anything or anybody. Additionally, we feel emotionally unstable, less desirable, less valued, unworthy, wounded and the emotions continue to evolve. Based on the experience that placed you there psychologically, you sit down in the state of not making the mark. What we must realize is the circumstance and situation that caused the psychological trauma for you emotionally feeling like damaged goods is in the mind. This means we have the ability to change the mind set and to reverse the emotions that come attached to the distressing event that invaded our life at a point we did not have the ability to cope with reality.

As adults, we do not always realize we are living our life as if we are damaged goods. It is common for us to assume we cannot live outside of what someone said to us or did to us. Let me serve you notice "It's not True." You have the ability to live beyond and aside from what someone did or said to you. It is important to confront the emotions you feel and get them under control. Getting your emotions under control is vital for you to carry out the purpose you were born to fulfill. Think about the following areas and how they may apply to you.

- *An insecurely attached style of parenting*
- *Your decisions are made on labels place on you from your past*
- *You have an issue with trusting*
- *Your disposition is mean and bitter*
- *You are very defensive about everything*
- *You have difficulty being yourself*
- *In relationships you are the one who always leaves*
- *You expect and demand from people beyond what they have the capacity to fulfill, regardless of ability*

If you can apply any of the above items to your life or you can admit you are or have been that person at one time or another, it is a result of feeling like you are damaged goods. Yes, life can inflict us with some undesirable situations and cause us to feel some very detrimental emotions. The emotions sometimes linger for long periods of time and for some others a lifetime. I want to encourage you; you can overcome emotional trauma by first facing you have an emotional trauma that has impacted your life in such a way you are feeling inadequate and useless.

God is faithful and promises us the gift of life if we will only believe and trust him. *John 10:10* says, *"I am come that they might have life, and that they might have it more abundantly."* "More abundantly" means we have a superabundance of a thing. An abundant life is a life in its abounding fullness of joy and strength of mind, body and soul. **1 Corinthians 7:26** – Because of the present crisis, I think that it is good for a man to remain as he is.
I Peter 3:13-15 says, *"Who is going to harm you if you are eager to do good? [14] But even if you should suffer for what is right, you are blessed.* *"Do not fear their threats; do not be frightened.*

[15] *But in your hearts revere Christ as Lord."* We must remember, when a person says or does something that bruises our emotions it does remove the ability and the capacity for us to be good and do good. We must manage how we allow others to control who we are as individuals and how we contribute to our life and life's purpose. We cannot allow ourselves to live in fear nor be threatened by the actions of people who do not value who we are in Christ Jesus. The word confirms to us in *I Timothy* 1:7, *"For the Spirit God gave us does not make us timid, but gives us power, love and self-discipline."*

Take a new perspective on life. You need to affirm yourself daily with positive affirmations that build you up and give you energy to push toward your purpose. I do not care who did what or said what to make you feel dirty. You are good enough and you are more than a conquer. There may have been some past suffering, or you may experience some present suffering but there is a future for you and God will get the glory out of our life. **Romans 8:37b** says, *"If God be for us, who can be against us."* You must know that God is on your side always, in all situations and under all circumstances. **Romans 8:37** declares, ... *"we are more than conquers through Jesus Christ who loved us."* The blood of Jesus Christ was shed for us and there is no mistake, situation or act done in our life that is too hard for Him or that His blood does not cover. Do you know your good outweighs your bad?

Yes, sometimes bad things happen to good people and we do not always know how to handle the bad but know it all works together for your good. When we face challenges in life, it is an opportunity for us to learn and grow and become the better person and the one to carry out the purpose assigned to our life. In order for promise to be delivered, we must know our purpose. Consequently, there is sometimes pain amid the promises of God in our life. Remember stains do not remain they can be removed with the right approach and technique. Even though the good in your life or of your life is damaged, your life still has purpose. Each of us have felt at some point and time in our life as if we were used, betrayed, hurt, or maybe made to feel like a misfit, but God.

We all pass through this life as damaged goods and the repair work is ongoing. Reclaim your proper posture for your purpose, develop a new disposition for the position you were purpose to hold and change your attitude toward the person, the situation, or the circumstance that made you feel like you were damaged goods. You are WINNER, a VICTOR, and an OVERCOMER!!

Self-Evaluation- Damaged Goods

1. What life experience (s) have made you feel like you were not worthy or good enough?

_____

_____

_____

_____

_____

_____

2. Do you struggle with getting past the past and letting others in?

_____

_____

_____

_____

_____

_____

_____

_____

3. Do you struggle to celebrate the gift in you and the gift of you?

_____

_____

_____

_____

_____

_____

Grace Check:
If you have not already…

Can you find it in your heart to forgive and let it go? Search yourself deeply with this question and pen your true feelings. It will help you with healing.

_____

_____

_____

_____

_____

_____

_____

Jot the immediate thoughts that come to mind whereas feeling like **damaged goods** concerns you... then **JOURNAL** about each thought you jotted down. *(Jotting is a word or quick phrase- Journaling is writing complete thoughts about what you jotted)*

_____

_____

_____

_____

_____

_____

_____

_____

_____

_____

_____

_____

_____

_____

_____

_____

_____

_____

Chapter 8
THE GIFT

A gift is something given willingly and freely to someone without a payment or cost. A gift is also defined as a natural ability or talent, a notable capacity or endowment. Your gift will never change. **Romans 11:29** says, *"For God's gifts and his call are irrevocable."* It is important to know what your gift is and its functionality. It is possible for a gift to become just a talent because you only use it for self-gain or self-glory, however; your gift is designated for the purpose of impacting the lives of others. The gift of you - you are a gift! You were born with a natural ability, talent, capacity or endowment. It is up to you to know what the gift is and to maximize it. The unspoken gift – some of our gifts are unspoken. We never have to open our mouth, but our gifts are displayed with our hands or our mind. No one would ever know you possess the gift if they were waiting for you to verbalize it, however; whether voiced or not, the gift still remains the gift and it is on the inside of you.

Equally, there are gifts which are never uncovered or unwrapped. We carry them around each day of our life. We cover up the gift with shyness, insecurities, fear, etc. We are afraid to unwrap it and see what it truly has the ability, capacity, or potential to do. The gift is often protected unaware due to not wanting the gift to be infiltrated by a force you do not have the strength or wherewithal to manage, develop, or grow. We sit in rooms, crowds, congregations, offices, classrooms, conferences and never allow the gift to be unwrapped. We keep it wrapped for the fear of failure and not measuring up. The gift on the inside of you is a hidden treasure for which only you can fulfill and bring to manifestation in your life. The gift each of us possess is a treasure. It is valued and of great worth; it should be esteemed and regarded as rare and precious.

The gift in you is necessary and was designed to change someone's life for the better. The gift you carry is connected to the purpose you should be walking in; the purpose for your life is designed to impact the life of those that are assigned to your life and your life only.

Only you carry and have the gift in you and no one else can do it or execute it the way you can. Your gift is tied and connected to your destiny. Who you were born and destined to be is a direct link to the gift inside of you, stir up the gift in you? Consider your passion and the thing you enjoy doing the most. Think about what comes natural to you and it requires no effort, you do not get tired when you are doing it, you could do it all day and you could do it for free. The gift in you gets your juices flowing, it wakes you up at night, and it is a place of calmness when everything around you is chaotic. Search your heart, mind, and spirit and ensure you are connected to your gift and your gift is yielding fruit in your life.

Moreover, your gift borrows from your purpose in life. The thing you were born to do and do it well. Purpose is natural as is a gift and it does not have to be rehearsed. Purpose brings peace in your life and gives you a sense of belonging and provides a level of comfort like nothing else can or ever will.

Knowing your purpose and operating in it will liberate your life and cause you to not only exist, but it will allow you to live life to the fullest. Purpose brings definition to your life! Your wealth is in your purpose and your purpose is in you, your gift. It is simply who you are inside. I would like to encourage you to slay the giant of fear, rejection, and pain and conquer your purpose with courage and faith. No longer allow negative influences to control your life and the ability to live it out loud. Gifts come in all shapes, forms, and sizes but every gift is important and significant no matter who you are and what the gift is.

Your gift is like anything else… you need to nurture it. Feed your gift with positive affirmation daily. Do not allow negative experiences to deteriorate and perpetuate the process of your gift developing and being given life. Experiencing these aspects of pain in our life will cause us to be less vulnerable to connect, build relationships, be friendly, open to love and be loved. When you feel you do not have the ability to trust, you must trust God.

Proverbs 3: 5-6 says, *"Trust in the Lord with all your heart and lean not to your own understanding. In all your ways acknowledge Him and He shall direct your path. Allow God to direct and steer your life. God will never lead you wrong, nor will He ever leave or forsake you,"* **Hebrews 13:5** confirms. God will always provide us with clarity and give us warning signs and signals whenever people come into our life who is not trustworthy. Allow your heart to be healed by God. It is important to rid yourself of the unforgiveness if you are holding it for anyone. For as long as the unforgiveness is housed, purpose cannot be born, it cannot grow, and it cannot develop. Now is the time to nurture your gift and prepare it for the birthing process. Begin to place the necessary thing in your mind, your heart, and your spirit that will help you to nurture the gift on the inside of you. Give your gift the emotional and spiritual nutrients it needs to develop and grow in a healthy way. If you will prepare yourself for your purpose to be born, when delivered; purpose will have a healthy environment for which to flourish and continue to evolve over time in different aspects and on different platforms.

There is a purpose and reason for everything that happens in each of our lives. If you are reading this narrative you still have time to put the time in, nurture the gift in you so purpose can be born. Throughout the phases of life such as transitions, separations, divorce, death, opposition, rejection, abandonment, offense, brokenness, trust issues, and having expectations which may have been mis-guided; God has given you the opportunity to walk in and live out your purpose.

Grace is God's unmerited favor and it is never ending for as long as you live, the favor of God is available for you and to you. Your purpose is time neutral and it is available for you to walk in, live out and share with the world. It is up to you to make the decision to live life fully caring out what it is you were born to do. *Innovation* is a part of who we are. Each one of us is born with creativity to some degree. The creativity everyone possess is based on the purpose for which they were born. Your ability to be innovative aligns with the purpose and assignment on your life. Often, we desire to do what another person does or have what another person has. Because we each have a measure of purpose, creativity and innovation; we do not have to worry about another person's measure of giftedness. We each possess the innovation and creativity for the specific purpose for which we were designed and birthed to carry out. When we are functioning in our gift, creativity and purpose, we have a feeling of freedom and we feel at peace.

Think about it for a minute, when a person is doing what it is, they love to do without limits, restrictions, parameters, and constraints; they are at their best and the happiest. The gift in us is functional at any time, any place, and we can do it on a whim because we are born to do it. We are never called or challenged to do anything for which we are not equipped or purposed to do. Being functional in your God given gift is a required functionality to impact the world and the kingdom of God. You matter and it matters when your gift is not functional and operating for the purpose for which you were designed. There are people depending on you to do what it is you were born to do. Think of all the times you did not do a "thing" because you allowed the opinion or perspective of someone else to derail you.

Also, think about the person or persons who missed out on benefiting from your gift. You are destined for greatness when you function, flow, and operate in your purpose. Transactional is the gift each of us carry. Each time we do what is in our personhood, we transfer our purpose and we impact a life. What an amazing opportunity to simply be you and make a different in the lives of other people. It is such a rewarding and amazing feeling.

Please do not allow the core of who you are to be distracted nor allow your gift to be aborted. Trust the plan of God for your life because he knows the plans and purpose, he has for you and only you. **Jeremiah 29:11** says, *"For I know the plans I have for you,"* *declares the Lord, "plans to prosper you and not to harm you, plans to give you hope and a future."* **Jeremiah 32:10** declares, *"great are your purposes and mighty are your deeds. Your eyes are open to the ways of all mankind; you reward each person according to their conduct and as their deeds deserve."* Job 42:2 confirms, "I know that you can do all things; no purpose of yours can be thwarted."

Jot the immediate thoughts that come to mind concerning your **gift** …
then **JOURNAL** about each thought you jotted down. *(Jotting is a word or quick phrase- Journaling is writing complete thoughts about what you jotted)*

_____

_____

_____

_____

_____

_____

_____

_____

_____

_____

_____

_____

_____

_____

_____

_____

_____

_____

Chapter 9
TO SUM IT ALL UP...LESSON LEARNED

When our spirits have been broken, our emotions have to rebuild the tolerance to love, to trust, to forgive and release the emotions associated with the emotional trauma experienced. We must regain the balance from the effect of the imbalance and dysfunction in life our functionality.

You were created in the image of God for his good works! **Ephesians 2:10** – "*We are handiwork, created in Christ Jesus to do good works, which God prepared in advance for us to do.*" The scripture confirms God has us on his mind long before we were formed in our mothers womb. **Jeremiah 1:5** decrees, "*Before I formed you in the womb, I knew you, before you were born, I set you apart; I appointed you as a prophet to the nations.*" You were designed by the divine and you are set apart for his purpose in the earth. We often plan out what it is we think we want to do and how we want to do, but please consult with God.

The plan of the Lord is always the priority and we should flow with it and in it. **Proverbs 19:21** says, *"Many are the plans in a person's heart, but it is the LORD's purpose that prevails."* **Proverbs 20:5** says, *"The purposes of a person's heart are deep waters, but one who has insight draws them out."*

There are people placed in our path to help draw out the gift, the purpose, the potential, and the abilities inside of us for the purpose of impacting the life of others. We each have an amazing work to do in the earth, please do not miss the opportunity to walk in your purpose and exercise the gift in you. **Colossians 1:16** says, *"For in him all things were created: things in heaven and on earth, visible and invisible, whether thrones or powers or rulers or authorities; all things have been created through him and for him."*

It is never ever too late to do what you were born and purposed to do. **Psalm 33:11** confirms... *"But the plans of the Lord stands firm forever, the purposes of his heart through all generations."* Whatever you do please do not abort the gift. God is intentional about the purpose placed in each of us.

Psalm 138:8 says, *"The Lord will vindicate me; your love, Lord, endures forever- do not abandon the works of your hands"* There is still time and there is still work for you to do, birth your purpose. When we allow ourselves to be hidden behind the veil of life's issues and negative experiences; we live in darkness. The word of God declares we are royalty. **I Peter 2:9** says, *"But you are a chosen people, a royal priesthood, a holy nation, God's special possession. That you may declare the praises of him who called you our of darkness into his wonderful light."* Do not allow abandonment, fear, rejection, brokenness, trust, etc., to keep you in a place of darkness. Free yourself and let it all go. Forgive anyone who you feel has wronged and mistreated you. It may seem as if you are getting the short end of the stick, but I promise you will thank me later. The ability to forgive and free yourself of negative thoughts and feelings is liberating and it brings a state of peace in your life you have never experienced. When you stop and really think about when a person hurts your feelings, offends you, rejects you or whatever the instance may be; the person is often unaware of the degree to which they impact you. In many cases it is very unintentional. However, because we do not deal with our emotions appropriately, many times we receive it incorrectly or we handle it with emotions only. We never take the opportunity to really evaluate the who of the what and the how of the when. We just feel only!

Whatever area has impacted your life, face it, confront it, deal with your feelings and release your emotions out of incarceration. It truly requires you owning the feelings you have in the areas discussed in this book. It also requires you doing the work and putting in the time to regain your place of productivity in life. You have a purpose to walk in and live out. There is "POTENTIAL" in you! You have purpose, opportunity, talent and energy, new life, transparency and innovative ability. You are a legacy; you have POTENTIAL in you! Own it!

Jot the immediate thoughts that come to mind regarding nurturing your gift and allowing your purpose to be born... then **JOURNAL** about each thought you jotted down. *(Jotting is a word or quick phrase- Journaling is writing complete thoughts about what you jotted)*

_____

_____

_____

_____

_____

_____

_____

_____

_____

_____

_____

_____

_____

_____

_____

_____

_____

ABOUT THE AUTHOR...

 ***Bridgette P. Moody*** is a native of Arkansas born and raised, currently residing in Texas by way of Tennessee. She is an Executive Professional, a Business Owner, a Strategy Consultant, Music Artist, Speaker and Facilitator to name a few. She is the founder of Pen2Paper Workshops and Conferences. She holds a Bachelor of Science in Business Administration for which she received with honors.

Aside from all the above, Bridgette is an ordained minister for which she has been in ministry the past 30 years. She ministers across the country sharing the message of purpose of vision and the importance of knowing who you are in God for such a time as this to walk in the purpose and the plan of God for your life.

Finally, Bridgette is the mother of two adult sons and one adult daughter. She is also the grandmother of two granddaughters and one grandson.

Bridgette is passionate about the message of purpose, vision, and having a plan to carry out the purpose for which you were born. She has traveled extensively across the United States of America sharing this message of Pen2Paper and purpose. The project "Gift Aborted" is the fourth literary work published by Bridgette and another project is underway. She has been effective in helping many Pastors and ministries as well as individuals and business owners to break the mold and take their thought process of vision and purpose to a new place of thinking and strategy. She is affiliated with organizations and company's that provide a platform to help people align with the assignment on their life.

CONTACT INFORMATION

BOOKINGS: Book Bridgette Moody for any of the following:

- Motivational Speaker
- Conference Facilitator/Instructor
- Women's Retreat
- Strategy Management/Training

SOCIAL MEDIA: Bridgette Moody

Facebook | Instagram| Twitter |LinkedIn

Web: www.bridgettemoody.com **&** www.pen2paper.biz

Email: bridgette@bridgettemoody.com

All Authored books are available on website or via amazon.com

Mail Correspondence to:

Bridgette Moody
621 E. Princeton Drive #95
Princeton, TX 75407

Made in the USA
Lexington, KY
04 December 2019